PHASE 3 PUBLICATIONS

THE MUTUAL CONVO'S

KA. PARINASRI - MOHAMMED NIYAZ

(Phase 3 Publications / MUMBAI - CHENNAI - INDIA)

First Edition 2022 By - MOHAMMED NIYAZ AND KA. PARINASRI

Editors And Covers - MOHAMMED NIYAZ AND KA. PARINASRI

Contents

Foreword   vii

Preface   ix

Acknowledgements   xi

Prologue   xiii

Prologue 2   xv

THE MUTUAL CONVO'S

THE MUTUAL CONVO'S

THE MUTUAL CONVO'S

THE MUTUAL CONVO'S

THE MUTUAL CONVO'S

THE MUTUAL CONVO'S

THE MUTUAL CONVO'S

THE MUTUAL CONVO'S

THE MUTUAL CONVO'S

THE MUTUAL CONVO'S

THE MUTUAL CONVO'S

THE MUTUAL CONVO'S

THE MUTUAL CONVO'S

THE MUTUAL CONVO'S

THE MUTUAL CONVO'S

THE MUTUAL CONVO'S

THE MUTUAL CONVO'S

THE MUTUAL CONVO'S

THE MUTUAL CONVO'S

Foreword

A set of pages can be seen filled up with so many unknown and unspoken emotions hidden with the rust of truth. Here a frankly speaking term considers under divisions of multiple regions. One after the another replies and relies to the aftermath of the said versions upfrontly with segments of sparkle. **"The Mutual Convo's"** under **Phase 3 Publications** is a combination of mixed feelings penned by the duos, we present you a variations of different genres as well taste of feelings hidden under the truth that lies beneath the minds and thoughts of the same.

Preface

Acknowledgements

There is a rare conversation which can be relate in terms of fruitful gestures in those acknowledged bonds. But this may mark the rest of the best interfaces of mixing true intentions through the soulful vibes. **"The Mutual Convo's"** Under **Phase 3 Publications** by **KA. Parinasri** And **Mohammed Niyaz respectively.** This marks the **third sequel collaboration solo copy** after "The Ink They Shared Through The Words" And "The Collaborate Authors" of the **most successful collaboration compilers duo in the writing industry** and for letting us pouring down the wonderful thoughts under this book. We hope our readers have a great time out there with the same.

Prologue

KA. PARINASRI
(AUTHOR & FOUNDER)

KA. PARINASRI
She is a passionate writer from Chennai. Writing makes
her pressure go away. She had played the role of co-author for
more than 100+, Compiled 30 Books, And she is compiling
many more which is on progress!

Her 1st and foremost book as a compiler was 'MY PEN FLOWS MY PAPER RECEIVES'
Wish You Were My Better Half is one of her favourite anthology - which hit the award for compiling it within 24 hours.
Well, She would like to thank her Loved ones for supporting her rather than stopping her from what she wanted to do! For being the main reason for achieving her dream.
She believes that anyone could hurt her, But never her books could!!
She had published 2 solo books.
1. JP: The Blessed Better Half
2. The Utmost Desire of Roaring Shout
Her Dual books
1. The Ink They Shared Through Words
2. The Collaborate Authors

Prologue 2

MOHAMMED NIYAZ
(AUTHOR & FOUNDER)

Mohammed Niyaz hails from Mumbai - The City Of Dreams. He often loves to write poetries and short music video stories for his own youtube channel. Apart from this Mohammed is currently working on his upcoming anthologies, as well writing poetries since 2013. You can find him on facebook/mohammed niyaz as well on instagram @niyazsks.

THE MUTUAL CONVO'S

Healing isn't that easy tho,

and in her situation, none can seriously heal for now!

Well somehow she is holding up,

and seriously she doesn't know when things are gonna end.

- KA. PARINASRI

There is still so many things surrounding

her with well versed effects,

yet she's on a verge of remaining uptil undefeated.

- MOHAMMED NIYAZ

THE MUTUAL CONVO'S

Friend:

*Your current circumstance is so painful to hear.... no you
don't deserve this pain!*

Me:

lol, I don't deserve but see what God is giving me?

- KA. PARINASRI

Friend:

Are You afraid of being alone to those different standstills?

Me:

Maybe! But i won't be fearing to

anything else rather than one and only me.

- MOHAMMED NIYAZ

THE MUTUAL CONVO'S

Well,

Hoping that before their expiry date

God will show some concern and shower some good vibes on them.

- KA. PARINASRI

It may or can be the best of the ever test

that will give a sure some thrill.

- MOHAMMED NIYAZ

THE MUTUAL CONVO'S

Umm. In their life,

They are just surrounded by plenty of misunderstanding people,

Uhh, and with many problems creators!!

- KA. PARINASRI

And they aren't a content creator,

they are the biggest chapters

of so called misunderstandings syllabus.

- MOHAMMED NIYAZ

THE MUTUAL CONVO'S

Instead of choosing to murder me before, my last day,

I would prefer to live until death hits me

Never mind what am leading to happy or sad,

But yet just gonna live this life

just for the purpose, I was born!

- KA. PARINASRI

Being a human it feels good to be

surrounded by birth, a worth match making

that lies within me or my breathing soul.

- MOHAMMED NIYAZ

THE MUTUAL CONVO'S

Even tho she pretends to show off she feels

like being in a quite good occurrence,

Well again the new problem arises and she is dying!

- KA. PARINASRI

Lying and reliving isn't the correct change,

let it go off and be the old one to bring in the group of avenge.

- MOHAMMED NIYAZ

THE MUTUAL CONVO'S

So sometimes all you need to do is!

Get lost with all your memories!

Everything will fade away,

but not the picture unless you allow them to move away from you!

- KA. PARINASRI

It's a bunch of screenshots that keeps

revind on your minds of reels,

which cannot be deleted yet remains

restore in the cage of tomorrow's stage.

- MOHAMMED NIYAZ

THE MUTUAL CONVO'S

Well, I don't understand why God only chooses us?

for showering all the hurtful and sad things.

Just bez we are being strong and facing all the situations with guts?

But yet how long will you just shower hurtful days?

instead of fruitful days??...

- KA. PARINASRI

When bad comes to you,

you must go with the patience you have,

rather than hurting yourselves you could be able to

move to a new and newer coast of fewer blissful rays.

- MOHAMMED NIYAZ

THE MUTUAL CONVO'S

When will the time turn for you to understand her?

When will you realise how much she loves and cares about you?

She wishes for somehow he would realise this before she leaves the world!

- KA. PARINASRI

There's enough time for you to bring back into her lost senses,

do get her back she's waiting for you since timeless lines ever,

or it will be a worth of losing her for generations forever.

- MOHAMMED NIYAZ

THE MUTUAL CONVO'S

Life is a mess, not sure what to do

Ongoing with so much of downs.

Hope is still alive but,

Yet just surrounded by losing the hope tho!

- KA. PARINASRI

Did i choosed life or the problems for myself alone?

Questions and answers is a must for me to revise the efficiency

of being right or way back again!

- MOHAMMED NIYAZ

THE MUTUAL CONVO'S

*Well at times it feels like enough is enough of handling all the
sufferings,*

*Ummm.. too tired of handling all and getting under the
hurtful trap*

Guess, god only loves to give me alone!

- KA. PARINASRI

*I stood at a ways of decisions to end up myself in a word of
none*

But hey how can't I be such careless to be selfish

against taking my own life because of them?

- MOHAMMED NIYAZ

THE MUTUAL CONVO'S

You always occurred about your world

And the ones who are included in it!

But you never realised that you are my one and the only world!

And I just live this life for you!

- KA. PARINASRI

I couldn't thought me without you, only priority of me was you

And you at the end was about to celebrate

thoughts of your own written vibes!

- MOHAMMED NIYAZ

THE MUTUAL CONVO'S

Well for the very 1st time,

I didn't miss You!!

Uhh, I won't say you never crossed my mind,

You did but just for a fraction of a second!!

- KA. PARINASRI

But thanks to you for being so good at the point of our attraction,

which stays in a clear state of something

newer than curious section!

- MOHAMMED NIYAZ

THE MUTUAL CONVO'S

Friend replies to the WhatsApp status:

Amazing yaar keep rocking the same way with your passion and keep adding many more books to your book collection!

Me: Hahan Thanks

What is gonna happen by just rocking in it!

When my real life has been to Zero?

- KA. PARINASRI

Friend Replies To The WhatsApp Status:

Remember A Zero Has A Worth In Making 10 In Thousands And Lacs Into Billions,

Since You Are One Of Millennium!

Me: A friend Like you Is a region of blessed session.

MOHAMMED NIYAZ

THE MUTUAL CONVO'S

Them:

Just have a hope that you would pass through this hurtful phase of life.

They are just temporary!!

Me:

Lol, nothing is being temporary in our life!

Well, only we are temporary!!

- KA. PARINASRI

Them:

No days or minutes will lasts until they

leave you by themselves away.

Me:

Only problems for can be permanently

designated when people like me relates to the then!

- MOHAMMED NIYAZ

THE MUTUAL CONVO'S

According to everyone they were meant to be TOGETHER FOREVER!!

who knows according to GOD'S SCRIPT

they were just meant to be together for a while?

- KA. PARINASRI

It looked like a scenario of a movie's rhyme,

but at last Romeo became juliet's worth worst villain for her rest life!

- MOHAMMED NIYAZ

THE MUTUAL CONVO'S

Tired, sick of everything! Plenty and plenty of waste bitchy contacts!

And then when I looked back I just found nothing, also realized there is not even a single pure Soul waiting for me to show back the caree! And you proved to me you're just a waste and a temporary one ever! You lost your worthy imp place in my life!

- KA. PARINASRI

I may reach within you to teach a lessons of multiple times,

but not again and again to repeat the points in

order of the replacement sometimes.

- MOHAMMED NIYAZ

THE MUTUAL CONVO'S

Stop moving in your life with others' opinions

Hold on a second and think about the other view

don't just blindly believe or don't take the next step with whatever the people whom u like say.

- KA. PARINASRI

Stay until what comes for you and watch what keeps

exiting excluding you! You will find a

clear picture of reverse verbs into times true!

- MOHAMMED NIYAZ

THE MUTUAL CONVO'S

He mostly occurs this isn't the satisfying life.

As if she is satisfied living the life with him?

- KA. PARINASRI

She isn't in a way to connect through his charm,

he either couldn't find a way to be in her lists of thinking plan!

- MOHAMMED NIYAZ